Loving You

Tom Hipps

Order this book online at www.trafford.com
or email orders@trafford.com

Most Trafford titles are also available at major online book retailers.

Printed in Victoria, BC, Canada.

ISBN: 978-1-4269-1638-0 (sc)

*Our mission is to efficiently provide the world's finest, most comprehensive
book publishing service, enabling every author to experience success.
To find out how to publish your book, your way, and have it available
worldwide, visit us online at www.trafford.com*

Trafford rev. 9/22/2010

 www.trafford.com

North America & international
toll-free: 1 888 232 4444 (USA & Canada)
phone: 250 383 6864 • fax: 812 355 4082

DEAR READER:

"Love is a many splendored thing," the words from a popular song proclaim. And for centuries, men and women the world over have been trying to capture it's elusive essence, and bask in that splendor.

Over the years many attempts have been made to define love. The Bible says simply that, "God is love." Thus love is said to take on the omnipotent character and nature of this supreme being that we call God. The Apostle Paul says that love lives forever and that it is the greatest thing in the world.

Perhaps it is not possible to define love, for in the process of defining it we can only limit it and thus demean it. Maybe all that we can say and should say about love is, in the words of a recent poem, "Love is. That is all we really do know and all we need to know."

So many poems have been written about love already that it seems like overkill to add any m ore on the subject. In such a circumstance, the challenge to the poet is to try and say something somewhat new; or, at least, try to present a slightly different view of this old familiar subject.

In the love poems that I have selected for this collection, I have attempted to show some of the multiple personalities of love; some of it's many changing faces and it's ever evolving nature.

It is my hope that as you read these poems, some of them will illicit from you the response: "You know, I had never thought of it quite like that before." If I can just get you to think of love in a different light; and help you discover some new thought or twist of meaning—I will be successful in my efforts and most pleased.

-- Tom Hipps

CONTENTS

1. Loving You   1
2. Quest   3
3. Welcome   4
4. Introduction   5
5. Openings   6
6. Where The Wind Blows   7
7. Once In A Blue Moon   8
8. Into My Sometime   9
9. There Was A Man   10
10. My Friend   13
11. Love Lay   14
12. Love Country   15
13. Dear Love   16
14. Love Walk   18
15. The Shadows of the Glen   19
16. Lament L' Amour   20
17. Speaking of Love   22
18. Ole Mister Moon   24
19. Lizard Love   26
20. Declaration of Dependence   28
21. Song of Love   29
22. Forever Dreams   30
23. A Penny's Worth   31
24. To Make A Rainbow   32
25. When My Love   33
26. I Was Jealous   35
27. Touchings   37
28. Dear One   38
29. My Very Best Friend   39
30. Somewhere   41
31. My Lovely Maid   42
32. We Two Ships   43
33. Masterpiece   45
34. To A Beautiful Face   46
35. Love Will Remember   47
36. I Will Write Your Name   48
37. How Do I Say Love?   49

38. The Me I See In You   50
39. I Must Die   51
40. Love Hunger   52
41. Banquet   53
42. My Eyes   55
43. Love's Grammar   57
44. I Built A Dream   59
45. Love Key   60
46. The Face That Launched A Thousand Ships   61
47. Color This Poem You   62
48. You Are Poetry   63
49. Discovery   64
50. Little Gypsy   65
51. Love Matter   66
52. She Came Dancing   67
53. Love's December   68
54. Hide and Seek   69
55. So Many Girls   71
56. So Many Fish   73
57. The Thing About Love   74
58. The Heart's Mind   75
59. Could It Be?   76
60. My Two Eyes   78
61. My Dreams   79
62. The Gift   80
63. Love?   82
64. Dogwood Dreams   84
65. Le Petite Morte   87
66. I Courted Love   89
67. The Night Beckons   90
68. It Follows   91
69. Step Softly My Heart   92
70. Sybil's Loves   93
71. Love Crumbs   95
72. Why?   96
73. Never To Ever Be Lonely   98
74. Soft   100
75. Game of Love   101
76. Love Feast   102
77. To Love is to Seek   103
78. Love Math   105

79. Lovely Lady Poetry   107
80. On the House   109
81. The Poet Quixotic   110
82. Poetry is Life   111
83. My Love Went Walking   112
84. Love Is A Bridge   114
85. Love Addition   115
86. My Friend   116
87. A Softer Song   117
88. Love Is A Morning   118
89. Dreambird   119
90. Where Love Hangs It's Hat   120
91. Forever Is A Song   121
92. My Heart's Young Road   122
93. Love Is Poetry   123
94. Love Is Blind   124

LOVING YOU

Loving your voice
I have heard you speak
with the tongue of a
thousand women;
have listened to your
gentle love whisperings
in the wind's soft breathings;
have slept peacefully,
soothed by your lullabye
in the night rain;
have awakened to your song
in the throats of a
million songbirds, greeting
the new born day with joy.
Loving you
I have seen you gather
in a crowd of women;
have watched you move
in a field of bright flowers,
plucking the first blossoms
of sun;
have seen you clothe yourself
in moonlight, plucking the
silver moonbud for your hair.
Loving you
I see you,
I watch you,
I hear you;
in the smile,

in the face,
in the voice
of a million women.

We love the things we love for what they are.

--ROBERT FROST (1874-1963)
American poet

QUEST

I must try
with unskilled hands
and with words
so unrefined,
to grope for love
so hard to feel;
to seek for love
so hard to find.

WELCOME

Welcome into my dreams;
oh wont you please just step
inside?
For you, the door is open wide.
Here the skies are always blue,
and there's a rainbow just for you;
life is always what it seems,
in my dreams.
Welcome into my heart;
wont you please step right in–
side?
For you, the door is open wide.
Together we will share mirth and
song,
chase the weary blues along;
a fresh new day is eager to start,
in my heart.
Welcome into my poem;
Oh wont you please come on inside?
For you, the door is open wide.
We will share some lyrical lay,
just to pass the time of day;
life is one paean to poesy,
in my poetry.
Welcome into my life;
for you, the door is open wide
Please do come in!
Just step inside.....

INTRODUCTION

When two eyes meet two eyes,
they say, "Hello."
The ABC's of the birds and the bees,
the yes and the no, they know.
When two hearts meet,
their rhythmic beat
keeps perfect time.
The lyric verse
of their universe,
sets reason to their rhyme.
When one soul meets another soul
and asks, "Do you?"
This is merely an introduction
to answering, "Yes. I do!"

OPENINGS

In forever land creation opens
A quiet hand and it's spring again,
A time for openings of closings
Of welcome windows whispering
Newborn breathings
Awakening awareness of a
Soft succulence seeing seeming.
Time that teller of tales
Has something to say:
The world's adolescence awe–full
Beginnings ritual renewing
In the heart a silent spirit
House–keeping opens a window
Inhaling fresh gladness.
Listen! Silence, singer of
Sweet songs is music making
All beings busy becoming life's miracle
Alive growing springs into being.
Everywhere are happenings:
Emergings coming blushing shyly
Stepping forth love opens a door
Exhulting exhaling stale stiflings.
Let everything now know
Love is a moment opening and
Love opens all . . . . .

WHERE THE WIND BLOWS

Where the wind blows
there my heart goes
skipping through fields of delight;
Where the stars shine
there my soul pines
scenting the dews of the night;
Where the flower blooms
in my heart there's no room
for feelings of sadness and pain;
And wherever you are
be it near or afar
my love will ever remain.

ONCE IN A BLUE MOON

Once in a blue moon
someone like you
comes along;
now under a new moon
someone like me
sings a new song;
a song of old yesterdays gone,
a song of young tomorrows,
young dreams to live on.
Now there's no more blue moon
but a full moon above;
smiles on a new someone
so full of new love.

INTO MY SOMETIME

Into my sometime
you came,
a face
without a frame;
you signed your name
on my heart,
then left
without a parting word.
Into my someday
you flew,
a song
from the blue;
my heart sang songs
it never knew;
then one day,
you flew away.
Into my somehow
you go,
my heart
will alone know where;
a song of love to sing
on some future spring;
into my someway
you'll stay.
Into my someday,
into   my sometime,
you'll go:
I know!
I know!

THERE WAS A MAN

Once
there was a man who said:
"I love "you!"
It's true!
I do!
And to prove that I do
I'm willing to give
my life to you!"
Once
there was a woman who said:
"Love you I don't!
Yes! That's true!
And just to prove it,
I won't give
my life to you!"
Once
there was a man who said
"You can love me
if you only try!
Please tell me you will,
don't make me cry!"
Once
there was a woman who said*
"No! I won't try!
And I won't tell you why!
I'd rather be dead!
Just go on and cry
you big baby!"
Once

10

there was a man who cried:
"Why won't you try
to love me?
Why? Why? Why?
You could if you would,
I know I'm good
and worth loving!"
Once
there; was a woman who cried:
"I don't wish to; discuss it!
I don't care how good you are!
I'm through talking to you!
Go on and get out
if you do really love me!"

Once
there was a man
who walked away!
Who sadly turned that day
from the one he loved!
From the face he loved!
From the voice he loved!
Once
there was a woman
who walked away!
Who gladly turned away
from the one who said:
"I love you!"
From the face that said:

"I love you!"
From the voice that cried:

"I love you!"
Once
there was a man
who took a name,
a voice, a face,
opened the door of his heart
and gently placed them there
where loving hands of care
could keep them in a safe place.
Once
there was a woman
who took a name,
a voice, a face,
opened a door marked Past,
there bound them fast!
Then in the cold tomb
she locked them in!
Once
there was a woman
who wrote:
"Goodbye!"
Once
there was a man
who cried!
Once
there was someone
who loved!
Once
there was someone
who died!

MY FRIEND

My friend
the wind, says:
"love is more a touching
than a holding;
more a feeling
than a knowing;
more a glimpsing
than a seeing."
My friend
the sun says:
"love is both an
awakening and sleeping;
both a beginning and
an ending,
a coming and going."
My friend
the rain says:
"love is stillness
yet forever moving;
love is sitting
yet always standing;
love is receiving
yet never stops giving."
My friend
the earth says:
"love is dying
but always living."

LOVE LAY

How have I loved thee?
Let me count the lays:
1, 2, 3, 4, 5, 6, 7, 8, 9, 10.....
How will I love you?
Let me count the ways:
sideways, doorways, alleyways, all ways...
When should I love you?
let me count the days:
Sunday, Monday, Tuesday, Wednesday, Thursday,
Friday, Saturday, Funday....
How may I love you?
Let me count the mays:
Maisie, Maybell, Mayme, Mavis...
When will I love you?
Let me count my pay:
$$$$$$$$$$$$$$$$$$$$$$$$$
Why do I love you?
Let me have my say:

LOVE COUNTRY

Into the country of love
I travelled alone,
dying of hunger
I begged for food
but love only tossed
me a bone.
What am I a dog
to chew on a bone?
Into the desert of love
I wandered unknown,
thirsty and dry as
a hard baked stone;
"Just one drop of water,"
I begged,
"Or I will die!"
Overhead only vultures
filled the sky.

DEAR LOVE

Love,
I want to ask you
a thing or two:
do you demand the most
from those with the least
to give?
Why do you seek
the fullest life
from those who can barely live?
How can a beggar pay tax
on a fortune he's never had?
How come the rich get richer
and the poor get poorer
in love?
How can you demand what
one has so little of ?
What reason do you give for laying
your treasure at
the rich man's door?
What is your reason for throwing
only crumbs to feed the poor?
When will you care
for those who need you most?
When will you reach out
to the wretched of earth,
cursed from birth?
Where can those who need you go
when you treat them so?
In this tragic tale

of too little much too late,
how can a man guard against hate ?

LOVE WALK

When love walks
upon the heart,
it leaves its' footprints
there for all to see;
When love talks
to the heart,
It's voice is heard,
it speaks without
a word.

THE SHADOWS OF THE GLEN

Oh I will go no more a courting
to the shadows of the glen,
I will go no more a meeting
my sweet love with tender greeting
in the shadows of the glen.
Oh I will sing no more in springtime
in the shadows of the glen,
I will sit no more a wooing,
no more romance pursuing
in the shadows of the glen.
Oh my cherished dreams have vanished
from the shadows of the glen;
but the tie that binds forever
in this life will never sever
my fondest recollections
for the shadows of the glen.
Oh my soul will long eternal
for the shadows of the glen;
and my thoughts will often wonder
as in memory I ponder
a very precious moment
from the shadows of the glen.
Oh I will cry no more
and sigh no more
in the shadows of the glen;
my sad heart is still repeating
muffled voices calm entreating
for that road so slowly stealing
through the shadows of the glen.

LAMENT L' AMOUR

Oft in the quiet of moonlight
when the sun slips over the hill,
and the voices of earth are silent
in the dawn of the twilight chill,
a soft breeze gently brushes
the fragrant evening air,
and the wind in humble reverence
whispers her evening prayer.
She kisses the stately branches
as she hurriedly moves along,
and dances with silent shadows
to the rhythms of her song;
with her mouth she breathes a greeting
to the watchful stars above,
while a young man quietly sitting
dreams only of his love.
He hears the night wind's greeting
and he feels her cool caress,
and with tangled tongue
he gropes for words
to form his heart's request:
"I come to this lake at evening
when the shadows of night start to fall
here I wait and quietly listen
to hear my sweetheart call;
I stare into the stillness
hoping to see her face,
praying that she will once again
come to this lonely place.

Oh gentle night wind on your journey
across the darkened sky,
I know that you may see her
from your pathway up so high;
will you tell her that I come here
to gaze at the heavens above
that every thought I whisper
is a prayerful thought of love?"
And still in the quiet of moonlight
when the sun has gone home to rest;
if you listen very carefully
you may hear this youth's request;
and if you by chance do hear him
entreat the heavens above,
you will know the nightwind still carries
his lonely cry of love

SPEAKING OF LOVE

I heard someone
speaking of love,
someone dressed in a silk suit
sporting a Botany tie;
someone who claimed to represent
"THE MOST HIGH."
But, I never heard a word he said;
I seek the living
not the dead!
I heard someone
speaking of love,
someone with a PHD
or some such pedigree
to call his own;
but I was hungry
and searching for more than
a bare bone to chew on;
So, I left well enough alone.
I heard someone
singing of love,
someone whining in an
inaudible tone;
someone casually inviting:
"Come on and sing along."
But, I didn't care to
face the music;
of someone crying in his beer.
I needed hope not fear.
I heard someone

speaking of love,
someone as cold as a stone;
someone lost in a crowd
and very much, alone;
Then I stopped to listen
to what he said:
"The only one who really knows
of love is dead!"

OLE MISTER MOON

Ole mister moon
keeps peeking at me,
winking a t me,
grinning at me;
ole mister moon
keeps laughing at me,
each time I am with you.
Ole mister moon
keeps spying on me,
cheating on me,
lying to me;
ole mister moon
keeps telling on me
every time I am with you.
Ole mister moon
keeps talking to me,
whispering to me,
shouting to me.
ole mister moon
keeps singing to me,
each time I am with you.
Ole mister moon
keeps walking with me,
playing with me,
praying with me;
ole mister moon
keeps staying with me
everytime I am with you.
Ole mister moon

keeps waiting with me,
sighing with me,
crying with me;
ole mister moon
keeps dying with me,
all the time I'm without you!

LIZARD LOVE

Love's
a tikklin'
in the gizzard,
that's as 'lusive
as a lizard,'
no matter where you scratch,
you never ever catch!
Love's
a tightnin'
in the tummy,
that wraps you up
like a mummy;
it knots you up so tight
you feel like a dummy!
Love is
a speck
in the eye,
as 'noying as a fly;
no matter how hard
you cry,
it just keeps
buzzin' by!
Love's.
a buzzin'
in the brain,
that's as 'ritable
as a pain;
in a place that's a no-no.
that makes you, want to go-go!

Love's
a hurtin'
in the heart;
that makes your stomach smart;
it tries to lecture you
on jest what you should do!
love's
a fire
in your seat;
it gives you such a start
you beat
a hot retreat!
Love's
a twitchin'
in your toe;
it tells your foot,
"Let's go:
It's the end of the show"
Love's
a wigglin,'
squirmin' word,
it is really for the birds;
for birds that are as looney,
as a goon who is gooney!

DECLARATION OF DEPENDENCE

These truths are self evident:
I need your lips
to put my thoughts into words.
I need your hand
to put feel into my touch.
I need your eyes
to focus my sight.
I need your arms
to fill my empty night.
I need your laugh
to make my sad heart sing.
I need your song
to serenade my spring.
I need your warm
to shut out my cold.
I need your young
to renew my old.
I need your heart
to strengthen my heart and soul.
I need your part
to complete my incomplete whole.
I need your faith
to keep my hope alive each day.
I need your hope
to sow dreams along my lifeway.
I need your life
that I may more fully live,
I need your love
so that I may freely give.

SONG OF LOVE

These people
sing their songs of love
and yet they can't compose;
a melody that she can play,
a simple song she knows.
These people
talk a lot of love,
and yet they never know;
what it takes to give her life,
and how to make her grow.
These people
like to write of love,
they give her praise and glory;
yet when they open up her book
they read a different story.
These people
like to play with love,
as if she were some game;
they wink and lie, they
drink and cry;
then they ask:
"What's in a name?"

FOREVER DREAMS

Her eyes planted
forever dreams
where gardens of moonlight grow;
promise fruits
from Eden streams
Where mannad waters flow.
Her lips sang
forever songs
where sunlight rivers, flow;
dream food
from ambrosia fields;
where trees of immortality grow.

A PENNY'S WORTH

If I had a penny's worth
of all the hate
masquerading as love;
there'd be enough
to clean all the cobwebs
out of the Great Above!
If I had a penny for each time
piety rushes to the rescue
waving its' sacred creeds;
making much ado about
someone in need;
and doing little
but beg and plead;
I'd be a very rich man indeed!

TO MAKE A RAINBOW

All it takes
to make a rainbow
is a little ray of sun,
shining through a raindrop
in the sky;
all it takes
to make a heaven
is a little gleam of blue,
dancing in the sunlight
of your eye.
All it takes
to make a rainbow
is a little drop of dew,
basking in the early morning sun;
all it takes
to make a heaven
is a little dream of you;
to fill my empty night
when day is done.

WHEN MY LOVE

When my love
makes love with her eyes,
a very flirtatious hue;
they beckon me:
"Come share
my dream of blue!"
When my love
makes love with her lips,
a very promiscuous red;
they implore me:
"Please come,
fill my empty bed!"
When my love
makes love with her voice,
a very lascivious gold;
it invites me:
"Come into my warm
come out of your cold!"
When my love
makes love in blue
I'm through;
(through and through).
When my love
makes love in red,
I'm dead;
(deader than dead)!

When my love
make s love in gold,
it's too late;
I'm sold!

I WAS JEALOUS

I was jealous of the wind
when I saw how he flirted with you;
how his anxious fingers
tugged at your dress,
playing with the smooth creases;
when I heard his voice whispering,
"Follow me",
how I wanted to be the wind
that I too might whisper
sweet nothings, sweet.
I was jealous of the sun
when I saw how he smiled at you,
saw the hot passion of his eye
devouring your helpless face;
when I saw him smother you,
with his hungry kiss;
how my lips burned with desire,
that I might taste your burning fire!
I was jealous of the moon
when I saw how he held you;
casting you under his magical spell,
drowning you in his moon magic.
when I saw him fill your mind
with fantasy;
I too dreamed that I might be
the story ship on your fabled sea.
I was jealous of the sky
when I saw him covering you;
saw how he protected you

from the heat of the day,
from the cold of the night;
when I saw him comfort you,
I too wanted to guard you,
and soothe you forever!
I was jealous of the stars
when I saw how they winked at you;
playfully promising you
a thousand things to wish upon;
when I saw you leaving me alone
with only my wishes three:
a hope, a dream, a love to be.
I was jealous of my eyes
when I saw them hypnotized
by your beauty;
transfixed too were my thoughts
and so obsessed by your presence;
my heart was enslaved
by the loveliness that is you;
that lives only in you.

TOUCHINGS

My eyes finger the golden nest
that rests above pools sky bright;
kindles magic fires of night.
I drink the liquid dream of blue light.
My thoughts scale soft mountain heights
where sweet scented fleshfruits feed;
hungry hopes explore warm worlds quiet,
taste bodies cool delights.
My dreams caress symmetries
sounding depths of shapes, shades,
feelings; planting touchings thirst.
Stillnesses embrace faces who plead,
"Kiss me:"
breathings who whisper, "Love me."

DEAR ONE

My dear one,
the main theme of this book is you;
from the first line to the last,
you will find this true.
The main plot of this story
is love; the plot and the theme
are one and the same,
and they both wear only one name:
You... You... O...U.....!
The leading character is you;
and I play a small bit part too;
each line and each page;
each stanza, each verse;
each poem in this book is all YOU!
From the first page to the last,
this is you;
from the beginning to the end,
it's still you;
somehow, some way or other,
there is just not another;
no one else will quite do;
but wonderful, marvellous;
georgeous, glorious;
lovely and beautiful you;
just you, my dearest one—
only Y...O...U...!

MY VERY BEST FRIEND

My eyes introduced you to my thoughts:
"Old pal, here is someone special
that you should meet;"
and my thought stuck out its' hand,
"Welcome friend, come on in and
take a seat; you are quite safe
in my cozy retreat;
come on inside, we will talk,
we will think; we will eat and
we will drink; and together we
will learn and get to know;
together we will love and
together live and grow..."
My thought presented you to my heart:
"My good friend, hello! This is one
very remarkable person, that I want
you to get to know."
And then my heart embraced you with
open arms and a welcome smile,
"Come on into my home, good friend,
come in and stay for awhile;
come in out of the cold,
come in where it is warm;
this is my own private place,
here you'll be safe from any harm.
Here we will hope and dream;
we will laugh and cry;
we'll go places, meet people,
and do lots of things together,

you and I..."
My heart introduced you to my love:
"Beloved, here is someone very
precious, someone who is very dear;
this is a very priceless human
being that I have here."
And my love invited you in with
my heart, "You have now found your
very own place; this is your own home
right here; come in and let us be
happy today, we will drink us a cup
of cheer; together we will love,
together we will live;
together we will receive and
together learn to give..."

SOMEWHERE

Somewhere you were there
A shadow of a dream
A promise of a prayer, still
In the early chill you were there
Breathing your warmth on the air.
Somewhere before my eyes
Could see your face
You filled a void of space,
Somewhere before some unknown poet
Dreamed the first rhyme,
Penned the first line,
You were there.
Somewhere beyond
The mountains of time,
Before the mists of rhyme
You were there,
A warm whisper on the wind,
A silence stirring in the air
Somewhere, You were there

MY LOVELY MAID

My lovely maid
grows a garden fair
that blooms in the forest
of her hair.
Where the songbirds sing
and the flowers swing
to the tune of the dancing air.
My lovely maid
owns a bright sunrise
that sleeps in the soft deep of her eyes.
Where jeweled light
set in pools of night
reflect a shy surprise.
My lovely maid
sings the brightest note
that skips as it slips
from her joyful throat.
A lyric laugh
that pens a rhyme
for the song the south wind wrote.

WE TWO SHIPS

We are two ships
passing in the night,
you and I;
and if by chance
we should catch the light
of the same star,
and looking at each other
see the same gleam
in each eye,
for a very precious moment
the secret of the ages
will be ours to command,
while we hold immortality
in the palm of our hand.

We are two boats
tossing on a turbulent sea,
you and me;
and if by accident
we should, sharing the same tide,
move closer together
and touch each other
in passing,
for a fleeting second,
for only one wondrous minute,
we will clasp the miracle
of the universe,
in the palm of our hand.

We are two vessels
drifting into eternity,
we;
cast off from different ports;
bound for different shores;
and if by circumstance,
if by mere chance
we should catch one glimpse
of each other's sail,
we will know of a certain
that we did not fail;
and for one brief bright moment,
two worlds met,
two universes embraced each other,
and time stood still.

MASTERPIECE

If I could use
an artist's brush
to paint on canvass
with a mater's touch
the birth of day
and the day at end,
I would capture there
in a perfect blend
of harmony
and quiet grace,
the eternal sunrise
of your face.

TO A BEAUTIFUL FACE

Your face is a song
no poet can sing
and in singing
see enough of
the spring blooming there,
beauty born of earth's harvest
no gleaner can reap,
of the sky
still an essence too high,
metaphors that dance,
lyrics that laugh
in an eye ...
of days,
of nights
where star-tossed rhythms play,
smiles that speak in sonnets
write of love's delights ...
you wear loveliness
with a grace
that becomes your face.

LOVE WILL REMEMBER

Love will remember a face,
whose smile planted a seed
in a cold waste,
and built a warm place
in the space of a moment ...
whose quiet fingers
plucked new lifelings
that flowered into singing,
    "love wills to live as
     live wants to love" .....
Love will remember two eyes
whose laugh kindled fires
in winter skies,
and lighted dancing stars
with soft hands
that touched the shores
of barren lands
with warm whisperings,
    "life wants to love as
     love wills to live" .....

I WILL WRITE YOUR NAME

I will write your name among the
stars, so that thousands of years
from today; some love lost poet
will look up into the sky,
and seeing your name written there,
he will remember my love for you,
and he will then love anew.
I will set your face up in the
heavens, to look down upon the
earth here below; so that mere
earthlings looking above,
may then know that this love
I feel today for you,
will live forever; and will give
light to all life on earth—
and thus will glorify love's birth.

HOW DO I SAY LOVE?

How do I say love?
How do I say blue?
You... You... Y... O... U...
How do I say lonely?
The very same way:
You... Y...O...U...
How do I feel heartache,
sorrow, and pain?
It is: You... and You....
and Y...O...U... again.
How do I spell love?
You... Y...O...U...
How do I write happy?
Only one word will do:
You...Y...O...U...
How do I know excitement,
wonder, and joy?
Only with you:
You... Y... O... U.....!

THE ME I SEE IN YOU

I do not want you,
I only want the me
I see in you;
the me I know in you
the me I want in you.

I do not need you,
I only need the me
I find in you;
the me I like in you;
the me I need in you.

I do not love you,
I only love the love
I feel in you;
the love I want in you;
the love I see in you;
the love I love in you.

For:

I want in you;
I need in you;
I know in you;
I see in you;
I live in you;
I love in you.

I MUST DIE

The ego screams, "I"!'
The self shouts, "MY!"
Before life can take root and live,
before love can bear fruit and give,
the ego, the self, the I,
must slowly wither and die.
In the fertile soil of
the soul's deep need,
love will plant her seed;
the loveseed will take root and grow,
that all life on earth may know:
so long as life will give,
so long will love live;
and love's fertile seed
will continue to feed
a hungry human race;
and love's ripe fruit
will firmly take root
that man may hope and dream,
and build his own small place
for love.

LOVE HUNGER

My thoughts hunger for you...
day and night they stalk about,
waiting, listening for your
voice; ready to pounce on any
careless word, hungering to feed
on any idea—setting it on
the table; throwing each
distasteful ought; relishing
each delicious naughty naught.
My hopes hunger for you...
drifting rudderless, aimlessly
on turbulent seas of chance;
fragile sails stuck waiting
for some wandering breeze,
to guide them to the storied
shores of romance; and there
along dreamland's fabled shore,
drop anchor forever more.
My eyes hunger for you...
Oh how they do idolize;
always on the go from head to toe;
feeding upon your beautiful body,
from your symphonic symmetry,
composing my poetry;
from each rhythmic line a verse:
a masterpiece titled: You...

BANQUET

You are my food,
I do not hunger;
I feed on the tenderness
of your touch;
I feast on the beauty
of your face;
I dine on the loveliness
that is you.

You are my wine,
I do not thirst;
I drink from the liquid
pool of your eyes;
I savor the rich bouquet
of your hair;
I sip your ripe cherry
berry lips.

You are my song,
I need no music;
your voice is a symphony
of a million songbirds;
mysterious melodies
come dancing on your words.

You are my poetry,
I need to rhyme;
your smile life's
springscript sonnet;
your laugh love's lyric line.

When I sit down
at your table to dine,
I feed on gourmet food,
and drink rare vintage wine.

MY EYES

My eyes fingers
touch your hand,
caressing each velvet inch,
feeling the texture of soft skin,
touching the fabric woven within.

My eyes lips
kiss your two lips,
tasting each drop of
ripe honeyfruit,
savoring your sweetness
from top branch to root.

My eyes hands
clasp your face,
holding you firmly in their embrace,
framing the soft loveliness,
the quiet grace
that is you.

My eyes thoughts
court your thoughts,
flirting with each shy hope,
teasing each bashful sigh;
making love with each dream
that sails the blue of your eye.

My eyes words
pen their words for you,
sonnets voicing their love
in poetic lays;
lyrics that laugh and dance,
singing your praise.

LOVE'S GRAMMAR

I was an improper noun
until you came,
giving me a proper name.

I was an inactive verb
in a passive mood,
until you erased the slate;
and wrote some being
into my state.

I was an abject adjective
with no subject to describe,
no meaning to transcribe;
but you had a cure to prescribe
when you became my scribe.

I was a pronoun with no person,
and no personality;
you gave me reason to rejoice,
when you came and gave me voice.

I was a dangling participle,
with no particle of purpose;
an indirect object
with no real objective;
a presumptious preposition
with only pretentious propositions;
a subordinate clause,
never getting any applause;

a parenthetical phrase
never winning any praise,
then you rephrased me.

I lived only in the past tense
until you corrected my present,
and rewrote my future.
I was a fragment of a sentence
with no subject,
condemned to remain incomplete;
with no aim and no purpose,
until you completed me.

I was in a lower case
until you capitalized me:
you dotted all my i's,
and crossed all my t's.

I BUILT A DREAM

I built a dream about you,
but my dream was made of clay;
when the raging waters of fear
came rushing in,
they washed my dream away.
I built a dream upon you,
but my dream was built on sand;
and when the angry waves
came crashing in,
my dream came tumbling down.
I built my dream around you,
but my dream was born of dust;
when the mad winds of doubt,
blew so wildly about,
they blew away with one
mighty gust.

LOVE KEY

I gave you the key to my heart;
you took the key, unlocked
the door, then walked in;
you sat down, kicked off
your shoes, and made yourself
comfortable in my own den.
Then in a very short time,
you went about arranging,
and rearranging; adding your
own special touches here and
there; opening a door and then
opening a window; letting in
some fresh air.
Then you staked out your claim,
and on the front door of my
heart, you wrote your own name;
for anyone, for everyone to see:
my heart was your very own
private property.

THE FACE THAT LAUNCHED A THOUSAND SHIPS

The face that launched a thousand ships
from Hellas' hallowed shores,
to set their sails for fated Troy
of epic Homerian lore,
history's hand could not erase
her noble lineage from your face.

The smile that scattered Egypt's sands
to make a hostile desert bloom,
that captured mighty Caesar's hand
and opened Pharoah's sacred tomb,
has endured time's erosive test
and on your face come home to rest.

COLOR THIS POEM YOU

Color this poem young,
something green newly sprung
from some hidden songspring,
a becoming thing.
Color this poem new,
something bright a dream of blue
bathing in infant light.
Color this poem soft, something
light borne aloft on mornings'
breeze,
a lovesong of sky and trees.
Color this poem love,
something unseen; a perfect blend
of green and blue,
color this poem you.

YOU ARE POETRY

You are the poem I cannot
write,
lost in the darkness of the
night
that fills me;
trapped in the maze of
memory that haunts me;
you are poetry.
You are the song I cannot
sing,
the winter's welcoming of
spring
that has passed me;
locked in the nightingale's
throbbing throat,
you are melody.
You are the life I cannot
live,
buried in the breast of
earth
that bore me;
a seed of spirit tossed on
the breath of time;
conceived in the womb of
living,
you are love.

DISCOVERY

When Columbus discovered America
he wrote a new history;
but when I sailed
the blue of your eyes,
I found immortality.

When the famous admiral
set ashore,
he saw an enchanted land;
but my heart explored a
magic world,
the moment I first
touched your hand.

LITTLE GYPSY

You say you'll be going away someday soon,
perhaps when the moon
hangs full like a silver pearl
your mind will fill with wandering ...
what unknown waits across the lonely hills?
A four leaf clover, a daffodill,
maybe a rainbow dream will
set your hungry heart wondering ...
why the wind whispers mysteries
of searchings for journeys happy end,
of meetings with new places, a new friend ...
smile on little gypsy moon of my dreams.

Wondering where you will go wandering
I await the moon's full face,
hoping to find rainbows lost in far away places,
golden lands beyond today ...
daffodill dreams and clover
speak softly to the night winds,
we talk of many things:
the faith of mountains, the hope of kinds,
and the shattered song only a fool sings ...
Shine on little gypsy, sun of my hope,
Sing on little gypsy, song of my night,
Smile on little gypsy moon of my dreams!

LOVE MATTER

You hallowed handfull of dust,
when you are in my arms,
my troubles just blow away;
suddenly it is spring again;
and we are walking through
the month of May.
You beautiful vessel of clay;
you marvellous molecule of matter;
oh how much you do matter to me.
Songbirds, green fields, blue
skies—are always beckoning me.
You awesome arsenal of atoms;
you stockpile of atomic energy;
you atomize me! You energize me!

SHE CAME DANCING

She came dancing by
in yellow,
skipping into a world
of green;
a fresh unplucked flower
she burst upon the scene,
slipping softly as a sunbeam
into my dream.
She came skipping along
in yellow,
dancing into a world
of green;
a soft fragrant blossom
freshening the scene,
tripping lightly as a March lamb
into my spring.

LOVE'S DECEMBER

In life's cold December
love will remember
soft rains of April,
bright blooms of May;
and in love's long winter
a warm wind may enter
its' young songs of springtime
awakening May.
In love's hungry season
when the heart knows
its' treason,
a cold-blooded loneliness
may conquer the will;
in the soul's time of wanting
when grim ghosts come haunting,
a welcome remembrance
will drive out the chill!

HIDE AND SEEK

Love likes to clown
and have her fun,
she never takes me seriously;
whenever I encounter love
she wants to play games with me.
No mater the time of the day,
never mind the day of the week,
when I meet love she always wants
to play a game of hide-and-seek.
She coaxes, "Please come play with me,
come seek and you will find!"
But if love can really be found,
then I am surely blind!
So, I close my eyes and I count to ten,
when I open my eyes, love is gone again;
I look in every nook and cranny,
in every hiding place,
but it's seldom ever I ever see
love's sweet lovely face.
I leave no stone unturned,
I look for her everywhere;
it makes no difference where I look
love just is not there.
But when I'm least expecting her
she jumps up right before my eyes;
she sticks her tongue out mocking me,
"Surprise!"
And when I start toward her,
reaching for her hand,

she's off in a flash taunting me,
"Catch me if you can!"
I chase her down the city street,
and down a country lane;
regardless how fast I run,
on love I never gain.
I run 'till I'm exhausted
then I drop down out of breath;
then love plops down right next to me,
and scares me half to death!
By the time I'm fully recovered
and just about to say, "Hi!"
Love's on her feet and off again,
waving to me, "Goodbye!"

SO MANY GIRLS

So many girls
named Linda,
but there's only one Linda
for me;
so many dreams
are named Linda,
and Linda's the one dream
for me!
So many faces
named Linda,
and Linda's the one face
I see;
so many warm smiles
named Linda,
and it's Linda who's smiling
for me!
So many lovers
named Linda,
but Linda's the one love
for me;
so many hopes
are named Linda;
and Linda's the one hope
for me!
So much happiness
named Linda,
and Linda's the one joy
for me;
so many sorrows
named Linda,

if it's sorrow,
then Linda it will be!
So many bright skies
named Linda,
and Linda's the rainbow
for me;
so many new dawns
named Linda,
and Linda's the sunrise
for me!
So many stars
are named Linda,
and it's Linda who's shining
on me;
so many full moons
named Linda,
and it's Linda's who's beaming
on me!
So many todays
named Linda,
and Linda's tomorrow
for me;
so many yesterdays
named Linda,
but Linda's the future
for me!
So many worlds
named Linda,
and Linda's the whole world
to me;
so much of heaven's
named Linda,
it's with Linda that I long
to be!

SO MANY FISH

So many fish
in the ocean,
I fear it's already
too late,
for all of those fickle fishes
have nibbled away
all my bait,
and left me alone with nothing
but a cold empty plate!
So many birds
in the heaven,
but all I can do now
is rage,
at all of those early bird hunters
who have locked them up tight
in their cage!
So many eggs
in the basket,
but it seems that
some slick slimey snake,
has swallowed them all and left me
with but one rotten egg
I can't break!
So many birds
in the heaven;
So many fish
in the sea;
So many eggs
in the basket:
one rotten egg omelette
for me!

THE THING ABOUT LOVE

Let the young
sing about love,
there's a thing about love:
only the young may sing
of a new awakening,
that brings springtime
to the heart!
Let the old
dream about love,
there's this thing about love:
only the old may cling
to love's eternal spring;
only those who've loved for long
know every verse of
love's old song!

THE HEART'S MIND

The heart
has a mind that's
all its' own,
it pays no heed
to what is known,
to what is unknown;
since it is blind
it cannot see
any clear reality.
It follows only a
rhythmic beat,
pressing on with
no retreat;
always ever on the go,
forward with life's
ebb and flow.

COULD IT BE?

The world
is full of people,
hundreds of people:
people wanting love,
people wanting to be loved,
people wanting to love;
why then
is there so little love?
Could it be
something in the wanting?
The world
is full of people,
thousands of people:
people waiting for love,
people waiting to be loved,
people waiting to love;
why then
is there so little love?
Could it be
something in the waiting?
The world
is full of people,
millions of people;
people needing love,
people needing to be loved,
people needing to love;
why then
is there so little love?
Could it be

something in the needing?
The world
is full of poets,
billions of poets:
writing poems of love,
writing poems for love,
writing poems from love;
why then
is there so little love?
Could it be
something lost in the translation
from thought to pen?
And then again,
could it be
somewhere in the transplantation
from page to heart?
Something?
Somewhere?
But, what could it be?

MY TWO EYES

My two eyes
are looking for two eyes,
to gaze into lovingly;
my two hands
reach out for two hands
to clasp and to hold
tenderly.
My two arms
are longing for two arms,
to fill this cold
emptiness;
My two lips
hunger for two lips
to meet in a warm
welcome kiss.
My two ears
are listening for a voice
to whisper:
"I love only you!"
And my sad heart
is lonely for a heart
to promise:

"I'll always be true!"

MY DREAMS

Oh that my dreams
were a reality,
that this unreal life
might a comfort be.
Often you flit
across my thoughts,
vanishing again in a moment.
How I wish that you would stay
and give my soul some
contentment.
If all of these nocturnal delights
that light the passions
on a dark winter night,
would take root
and forever lie
implanted in me!

THE GIFT

If I had one gift
that I could give,
the gift I would give
is that you might live:
as free as a breeze
that swims the air,
or sails the morning mist;
as free as the sun
that sweeps the sky,
then blows the world a kiss;
as free as a bird
that climbs the clouds,
and swings on the evening breeze;
as free as the flying fish that play
then sleep in a stormy sea.
I would give you the world
but it's easy to give
what we have not,
so I'll give what I've got:
a dream that is filled with you,
a hope that lives with you.
I would give you my life
if this life that I live
were mine to give;
so I give:
a heart that beats for you,
a breath that breathes for you.
I would give you immortality
if immortal I could be,

no more mortality;
but filled with the fullness of life
you would live,
filled with the joy of life
you could give.
The greatest gift
that one may give,
is what he cannot give;
the fullest life
that one may live,
is one he cannot live.

LOVE?

Love?
Can a man live?
Can a man live without loving?
Love is a hand opening,
that beckons: "Come!"
It is fingers clasping
that say: "Okay!"
It is a voice answering
"Yes I can!"
To a fear doubting
"No, I can't!"
It is a promise saying
"Yes, I will!"
To a doubt insisting
"No, I won't!"
Is it yesterday weeping for today?
Is it today waiting for the dawn?
Is it breath sighing for spirit?
Is it spirit seeking the soul?
Is it wisdom lost in the desert?
Is it hope climbing the mountain of heart?
Is it the mountain longing for the valley?
Is it the valley's dreaming of climbing?
Is it emptiness thirsting for fullness?
Is it fullness yearning to be drained?
Is it a father waiting for a son?
Is it a prodigal son sick for home?
Is it joy mourning for sadness?
Is it sorrow singing for joy?

Is it the creature's cry for the creator?
Is it man's quest for himself?
Is it was finding the is?
Is it is finding completeness in was?
Is it death gasping for life?
Is it life's dialogue with death?
Is it man's search for the womb?
Is it the womb yielding to the seed it bore?
Is it the marriage of love and hate?
Is it the wedding of life and death?
Is it one desiring to be two?
Is it two wanting to be one?
Is it endings looking for beginnings?
Is it questions seeking an answer?
Is it where discovering when?
Is it why unmasking what?
Is it never becoming ever?
Is it change growing to become?
Is it truth groping for fiction?
Is it fiction recording truth?
Is it earth's reaching for heaven?
Is it heaven's will to be free?
Love is a lifetime of living
between the joy of "Yes,"
and the sorrow of "No."
Can a man love without living?

DOGWOOD DREAMS

When dogwoods bloom
in Collins Park,
I think of that night
when alone in the dark
just we two,
I whispered:
"I love you!"
It was a time I won't forget;
early rain had fallen,
the grass was wet;
the sky was full of stars,
and a full moon above
could not match the fullness
of my love.
We sat in the damp of evening
looking over the lake,
all was calm
as if a storm would soon break;
inside me a volcano of emotion
came bursting out:
"I love you," I said.
Nature looked quietly on a scene
she'd seen a million times before,
the freshness of spring love
young and new;
and yet a story so often told.
it was no more new than old;
we sat under the dogwoods
and we talked,

then after some time
we got up and walked.
You were beautiful
in your dress of white,
the stars were envious
of the night
that held you so tightly.
And I
smitten by love
could only sigh;
I
full of feelings
never felt before,
knew only one thing
was true:
"I love you!"
I could not stop repeating
the same refrain,
over and over and over again:
"I love you!"
Words could not even start
to say what I felt in my heart.
My lips hungered to taste
the full blush of nature's bloom,
but my heart said:
"it would be a crime
beyond compare,
to steal one drop of sweetness there,
and rob that for which
there is no repair!"
And now,
when dogwoods bloom

in Collins Park,
alone
I sit in the dark
under the patient sky
and dream my
dreams of you.

LE PETITE MORTE

The French call love:
"the little death",
breathing pain and sorrow
with every breath;
some worldly-wise say
it's worth the cost,
after all it's better
"to have loved and lost";
romantics write poetic lays
singing to love
their songs of praise;
True Believers say that
God is love,
and as incomprehensible
as the heavens above.
Just what is love?
I wish that I knew;
perhaps it's different
for me and you?
Could it be for those
who do not know,
that love is just
the wish to grow
into love's likeness,
the will to be
always in love's company?
And for those who
have never known love,
maybe it's simply

the hoping to know?
Could this be love:
to dream
to hope
to live
to grow?
Maybe so?.....................

I COURTED LOVE

I courted love
as an anxious suitor
searches for romance,
she winked at me
with "come hither" eyes,
bidding me take a chance;
so stupid, I
the fool that I was
just "went along for the ride",
hoping that in
this love so rare,
I would win a faithful bride.
I stepped up to her
on the world's firm floor
and asked her for a dance,
I waltzed with her
around and around,
half-dazed and in a trance;
then in the darkness
of the night,
death claimed her
for his own;
love:
fickle,
faithless
she was to me
to leave me all alone!

THE NIGHT BECKONS

The night beckons seductively,
"Come to my arms my lonely boy;
for I am young,
there are songs to be sung,
and I have a million stars
to wish upon!"
The night whispers compellingly,
"Come to my arms my searching boy;
there's a full moon
to serenade;
plans to be laid,
and I have a million dreams
to build upon!"
Into the arms of my lover night
I take flight;
far from the demons
that stalk the day;
serenading a moon,
building on a dream
I'll stay.

IT FOLLOWS

It follows:
being no Indian-giver,
when he gave his heart freely
he gave it completely,
and he could not
and he would not
take it back;
not even when accompanied by a sign
reading: "Heart not wanted!
Return to rightful owner!"
It follows:
as the night the day,
love only once found her way
into the secret place
of his heart;
if she had shown her face,
called at his place
now and then,
she may have found
something there?
She may have discovered
something priceless,
something rare
beyond compare?

STEP SOFTLY MY HEART

Come swiftly my heart
while love is in her season,
let us dance and sing
while there is time
for mirth and song,
and while rhyme
has made peace with reason.
Beat slowly my heart
while love is in her bloom,
let us hope and dream
while there is place
for a special face,
while life still
has some breathing room.
Step softly my heart
while spring is in full flower,
while dreams are born
with each welcome morn,
while the gentle
is in power.
Come swiftly!
Beat slowly!
Step softly
my heart!

SYBIL'S LOVES

Sybil's in love
with Harry's hair,
she says:
just the thought of its' fire
keeps her warm
when the wild geese cry,
and yet,
there's a lack of old-fashioned ire,
Harry's too shy!
Sybil's in love
with Teddy's teeth,
she says:
they're so bright
she can find her way
in the night;
and yet,
it does grow kind of dull
just basking
in their light!
Sybil's in love
with Eddie's eyes,
she says:
they're so deep blue
they make her think of
everything true;
and yet,
Eddie often lies
with his eyes!
Sybil's in love
with Gary's grin,

she says:
the first glimmer
of a smile,
makes anything most
worthwhile;
and yet,
there's just a hint
of devilish guile!
Sybil's in love
with Nelson's nose,
she says:
it's real Romanic,
it always knows what
perfume she's wearin';
and yet,
often sets Nelson
to swearin'!
Sybil's in love
with Charley's chin,
she says:
it's sharper than a tack
and comes right to the point;
and yet,
when she wants to be alone
it's always butting in.
Sybil's in love
with Ernie's ears,
she says:
they're good as any rabbit's,
oh my, the things they hear;
and yet,
sometimes she'd rather be
more seen than heard!

LOVE CRUMBS

Love gave him only
her stale crumbs to eat,
then she held out her hand
begging bread;
"How can a man fed on crumbs
have strength to earn his bread?"
But she never heard a word
that he said.
Love gave him only
her left-over bones to eat,
then she held out her plate
demanding prime meat;
"How can a man who dines on bones
have any will to carry on?"
But she turned to him a deaf ear
she did not hear!
Love's got her crumbs
and plenty of bones for all
the hungry beggars of the earth
who daily come to call!

WHY?

Why do I love you?
I'm afraid that I don't know why.
But the sky loves Mother Earth;
and for what it may be worth,
Mother Earth also loves the sky.
I've never heard either one say why.
Do they really know why?
How about you, Do you? Do I?
Why do I love you?
Well, I don't know quite what to say.
But the day loves the night;
and the night really loves the day.
Do you think the night can truly say,
just why it loves the day?
No more than the day can say.
Can you? Can I say?
No way! It has always been this way.
Why do I love you? I wish I could see,
Why I love you and yet, you don't love me.
But the ocean loves the land, and the shore
loves the sea.
And whatever the reason,
season after season,
their love will always be.
Why do I love, you? I cannot answer why.
But the winter loves the spring,
and he has nothing to say;
about why this has always been this way.
On this question why, I doubt that spring

or winter could ever agree?
And yet this romance of winter and spring,
is a story told and retold;
of the old's love for the young.
Of the warm's care for the cold.
The cold's deep need for warmth;
the old's strong desire to again be young;
is an old song, so well known, and yet
so very new;
as is my love for you.
This is a song that has been, and forever
will be sung.
So long as tired old hearts stay young.

NEVER TO EVER BE LONELY

Never to have someone to go home to;
never to have someone waiting at home,
just for you;
never to have some special someone,
carve your name on a tree;
never is ever to be lonely!
Never to wait to hear the sound of one
very special voice;
that will make your sad soul dance;
will make your heart sing and rejoice!
Never to hear her whisper the words,
"Dearest one, I love you!"
Never is forever to be lonely!
Never to feel her soft hand pat you on
your back, with a: "Go on; you can do it!"
Never to feel her petite foot kick you in
your rear, saying: "Go on now; get to it!"
Never to feel wanted; to be needed;
by the tie that sets you free;
never is ever to be so lonely!
Never to look into two loving eyes,
gazing so lovingly at you;
never to look into those same loving eyes;
with your care and much longing, too!
Never to plant the seed of hope; and
harvest ripe dreamfruit bountifully;
never is forever and ever, to be lonely!
Never to hear the questions asked:
Do you? Will you?"

Never to whisper her your answer:
Yes, I will! Yes, I do!"
Never to pledge: "Till death we do part;"
and then vow: "I'll be true to thee!"
Never is ever and forever to be lonely!
Never to tightly clasp her hand;
with her hand holding on to you;
never to belong only to that special someone,
and have that very special someone,
belong to you only;
never to have ever known any of this;
well, this is what it means to be lonely!
Never ever to be loved; is to never
ever fully live!
This is to be oh so very lonely, only!

SOFT

I need your soft skin, to caress, to massage,
to touch.
I need your softness so much; so very much!
I need your soft lips, to taste your sweet;
this manna from heaven; such a treat to eat.
I need your soft ears, to whisper my
love poems to; to court you; to pursue you;
to pitch you my woo!
I need your soft eyes, to gaze into my eyes.
Your eyes to brighten my day;
and to enlighten my way!
I need your soft to break down my hard;
To make me more pliable;
as a human being, more viable.
I need your soft to soften my hard heart;
that I may be an integral part of the whole;
and not a lone, lonely separate part!

GAME OF LOVE

When love dons her mask behind home plate,
and calls out, "Play ball!"
I step timidly and warily up to the plate;
I know I am about to take a fall.
In this game of love, I never ever get a hit.
Why I never even get to first base.
It's strike one; strike two; and strike three;
I am out! I am down and out and
flat on my face!
Love has all the pitches; a fastball;
a change–up; and a wicked curve.
Why, the very nerve!
But love's very best pitch is the screwball;
it always catches me off guard.
Love really knows how to screw you.
And when she slips me her screw,
I fall hard.
When I play love, she always throws a no–
hitter. For me it's no hits; no runs; no
score. She is the winner and I am the loser.
For me this game of love is nothing more
than one great big bore!

LOVE FEAST

Your beautiful body, is prime filet mignon.
The perfect feast for these hungry eyes
to feed upon!
Your two ripe cherry berry lips,
for my two thirsty lips to sip,
your vintage Dom Perignon!
Upon your succulent breast,
my famished thoughts rest.
Until your tender thighs,
tempt my longing, starving eyes!
My mind massages your luscious legs!
Then it falls upon it's knees and begs!
Yes, my famished thoughts,
how they do savor the flavors of your
naughty naughts!
My eager thoughts thirsty tongue,
hungrily laps up your tart, tasty young!
So, I sing you a lovesick lovesong,
that I have never ever sung!
I do worship and pay homage to your
bountiful beYOUty!
In this short paean of praise,
that is my poetry!

TO LOVE IS TO SEEK

To love is to seek, though you may never
find.
To search always with a hungry heart;
with an endless questing mind.
In this, your lifelong love quest,
never to be content; never ever to rest!
To love is to search, with a hungry heart,
and a thirsting mind.
A thirst for wisdom that cannot be
quenched.
To seek out justice, in the midst of
so much injustice.
To search for understanding, amid
so much misunderstanding.
To press always onward, seeking
compassion and tolerance.
Even while surrounded by intolerance.
Always searching for wisdom;
in the middle of so much fear and ignorance.
Seeking, searching, looking everywhere;
for goodness; for kindness; for any
evidence of care.
To love, is a thankless, endless quest.
To seek. To search. To hope. To dream.
This priceless, precious love to find.
Always seeking with a hungry heart.
Always searching with a thirsting mind!
Looking for a clear, sharp insight;
in this blind darkness, that is

hatred's dark night!
To seek. .To search. .To hope. .To dream. . .
is to Love!

LOVE MATH

The old professor was a master
mathematician.
He once said to me, "You know friend,
love is just a math problem.
You know, it's just like one plus one
equals two. And now, two plus one
equals three.
That's with the addition of you and me.
Now if you add love to love; it
figures that you'll get more love.
There's no need to guess.
If you take love away from love;
or, when you subtract love from love;
then, buddy boy, you're gonna get
a whole lot less.'
Now if you multiply love by love,
and this is a math fact that's
always been so;
multiplication is a faster way of
addition; and this is a fact that
everyone should know!
So, what then can we say about love;
speaking quite naturally mathematically?
That love plus love always equals love.
Don't you my good friend agree?
Mathematically I say, without any
hesitation.
When you add love to love, then it's
love that's the answer to this equation.

So just what is it that this old world
needs the very most?
Why now, that's just as easy as 1,2,3.
The world desperately needs a course
in love. Of course, love that is
taught mathematically.
It is an uncontested fact;
we need to learn a lot better,
love's addition and multiplication
facts!

LOVELY LADY POETRY

My very first love rejected me
Many more women did the very same thing.
I was a flightless bird;
without a song to sing.
But, on one quite memorable day;
I met the one true love of my life.
I met a fair lass who could one day
become; my own devoted beloved wife.
Yes, my Lovely Lady Poetry;
she gave me so much of her time.
She taught me her rhythmic rhythms;
and all about poetic rhyme.
Then, Lady Poetry and I;
joined our hands and our hearts.
We vowed to live together;
and to truly love each other.
"Until death, we do part."
Ever since, Fair Lady Poetry and I;
have lived together;
and loved each other;
in perfect poetic harmony.
At long last, I have found
my one and only true love.
The fairest of the fair:
the Lovely Lady Poetry!

"My poets have the gift of joy,
they are the ones who can see things whole,
who can sense and comprehend the vast scheme
that has been designed for us..."
– – –Helen Hayes

ON THE HOUSE

Flesh of my flesh I give to you,
such a gift as this mortal is
heir to:
the poets' lot,
a paupers' plot;
hard muscle of mind,
lean tendon of thought
to fleshen bare bone;
strong sinew of soul
to feed on.
Blood of my blood I offer you,
this hemlock cup
a poet must sup;
dregs of dust
in this vessel of rust;
a sorcerers' brew,
this pot–luck stew.
Grapes of hope hang heavy
on the vine,
drowning despair in the
spirit lifting wine.
Sweat of my sweat,
bread of my brow;
bone of my bone
I break with you now.

THE POET QUIXOTIC

In these dark ages of the despotic,
in a world grown so chaotic,
you may dispense with the exotic,
send me a poet Quixotic.
In this savage time when tyranny
is the rule,
when freedom is the tyrants'
bloody tool,
send me just one Quixotic fool.

POETRY IS LIFE

Poetry is a dirty faced
barefoot boy,
sticking his tongue out
at the mirror.
Poetry is a freckle faced
pigtailed girl,
making faces at
Old Miss Fuddyduddy.
Poetry is life,
thumbing its' nose at death;
shouting with its' very last
breath: "You big bully!"

MY LOVE WENT WALKING

In a summer light
my love went walking,
went walking through the night
of a thousand suns . . .

On a winter night
my love came dreaming,
came dreaming from a
million milleniums . . .

In a young spring dew
my love skipped singing,
singing new songs
to a sleepy—eyed day . . .

On the autumn haze
my love went whistling,
whistling with the wind
as he froliced in play.

Love needs no song
to give her voice,
she calls in the wind,
"Rejoice! Rejoice!"

"There is a land of the living,
and a land of the dead; and the
bridge is love; the only sur–
vival, the only meaning. . ."
– – –Thornton Wilder

LOVE IS A BRIDGE

Love is a bridge:
the only path out of pain and strife;
the only way that leads from this
world of death, into a land of life.
Love is a bridge:
the only crossing that spans the
dark chasm of hate and fear;
the only safe refuge from the
angry storms,
that are always raging near.
Love is a bridge:
the only road that leads out of
darkness into light;
the only safe passage
into the springtime of a new day,
out of the dark winter of night.
Love is a bridge:
that guides us out of the
land of night,
into the newborn day;
from a world of darkness,
into a world of light;
from a kingdom of death,
into a kingdom of life— — —
the only hope; the only sur—
vival; the only meaning;
Love is the bridge. . . . .

LOVE ADDITION

I was the square root of nothing minus one,
until the day I met you.
After the introductory "Hello;"
and the customary, "How are you";
the judge ask each of us. "Do you?"
And each of us replied: "Yes, I do."
One plus one was two; a minus was made a plus;
when you were added to me;
and I was added to you;
and we two became just us.

MY FRIEND

Before the me, the my, and the I end;
you begin, my friend.
When the me, the my, and the I end;
you become my friend.
Where the me, the my, and the I cease to be;
you are free to be, my friend.
When the me, the my, and the I die;
I give that you may live as my friend.

A SOFTER SONG

A broken heart sings a softer song,
and understands well the tear-filled eye.
A shattered dream builds a stronger hope;
and hears the hurt in the silent cry.

LOVE IS A MORNING

Love is a morning
that nests atop hills of light;
like an eagle waiting;
to soar into flight;
as the sun's young rays
ascend the mountain's height.

Love is an evening
that sleeps in the valley of night;
as a morning glory, watching;
it plants it's roots in the deep;
and waits for the dawn
to write a new story.

DREAMBIRD

In love's green season;
when the heart toasts it's spring;
every dreambird from his nest;
lifts his voice to sing.
Oh sing dreambird, sing!
Welcome another spring.

In the heart's young season;
when love sprouts anew.
Every dreambird in his breast;
feels the call of spring blue.
Oh fly! Dreambird fly!
Lift your wing.
Embrace the sky!

WHERE LOVE HANGS IT'S HAT

Where love hangs it's hat;
the weary pilgrim finds a welcome mat.
A bite to eat; and a friendly chat.
A good give and take of this and that.
Where love pulls up a chair;
the lonely stranger is welcome there.
There is time to sit and talk a bit.
And pack away all worry and care.
Where love kicks off it's shoes;
the poor prodigal finds some welcome news.
Freedom to pick; and freedom to choose.
Time to laugh away those lonesome blues.

FOREVER IS A SONG

Forever is a song the morning sings;
when a sleeping world awakes to spring;
and life once again takes to wing.

Forever is a song the evening sings;
when winking lights start promising;

the gifts that a merry night may bring.

MY HEART'S YOUNG ROAD

My heart's young road reaches out for the sunshine
it's thirsty tongue lapping up the miles.
My heart's new day stretches up for the sunlight;
its' hungry mouth devouring the smiles.
My heart's fresh song climbs up for the tree tops;
its' childlike melody just learning to fly.
My heart's first love ascends the mountain;
its' childish trust embracing the sky.

My heart's youthful dream plants tender tomorrows;
explores virgin lands beyond restless seas.
My heart's eager hope plants welcoming rainbows;
on happy horizons; framing bright memories.

LOVE IS POETRY

So much of life is winter and spring;
So much of love is dance and sing.
So much of life is me and my;
So much of love is you and I.
So much of life is work and play;
So much of love is might and may.
So much of life is day and night;
So much of love is dark and light.
So much of life is try and cope;
So much of love is dream and hope.
So much of life is learn and know;
So much of love is plant and grow.
So much of life is hello and goodbye;
So much of love is laugh and cry.
So much of life is pain and joy;
So much of love is girl and boy.
So much of life is hit and miss;
So much of love is hug and kiss.
So much of life is aim and goal;
So much of love is heart and soul.
So much of life is old and new;
So much of laue is me and you.
So much of life is you and me;
So much of love is poetry.

LOVE IS BLIND

Love is blind we like to say;
but, is this really true?
True love; real love sees the faults;
the warts and all; but it sees the good too.
It is seeing someone as they really are;
and still being able to care;
that we attain true friendship;
and we find true love.
A find that is truly most rare.
A love that says:
"What you are; it does not matter.
I will always be there.
I care!"